WALLACE
AND GRACE
and the Lost Puppy

**READ & BLOOM BOOKS**

WALLACE AND GRACE

and the Lost Puppy

Heather Alexander
illustrated by Laura Zarrin

BLOOMSBURY
NEW YORK LONDON OXFORD NEW DELHI SYDNEY

For Sophia —H. A.

For Tracy, Renee, and Christina,
whose encouragement keeps me going
day after day —L. Z.

Text copyright © 2017 by Heather Alexander, LLC
Illustrations copyright © 2017 by Laura Zarrin

First published in the United States of America in September 2017
by Bloomsbury Children's Books
www.bloomsbury.com

Bloomsbury is a registered trademark of Bloomsbury Publishing Plc

For information about permission to reproduce selections from this book, write to
Permissions, Bloomsbury Children's Books, 1385 Broadway, New York, New York 10018
Bloomsbury books may be purchased for business or promotional use. For information on bulk purchases
please contact Macmillan Corporate and Premium Sales Department at specialmarkets@macmillan.com

Library of Congress Cataloging-in-Publication Data
available upon request
ISBN 978-1-68119-012-9 (hardcover)
ISBN 978-1-68119-571-1 (e-book) · ISBN 978-1-68119-572-8 (e-PDF)

Art created with Blackwing pencils and Photoshop
Typeset in Ampersand, Burbank, Century Schoolbook, and Roger
Book design by John Candell
Printed in China by C&C Offset Printing Co., Ltd., Shenzhen, Guangdong
1 3 5 7 9 10 8 6 4 2

All papers used by Bloomsbury Publishing, Inc., are natural, recyclable products
made from wood grown in well-managed forests. The manufacturing processes
conform to the environmental regulations of the country of origin.

Table of Contents

CHAPTER 1
Lost and Found

"I found it!" Grace held up the acorn.

"Great job!" cheered Wallace.

Grace flew to Wallace. He sat on a high branch. She carried the acorn in her beak.

"Is the acorn as big as my eye?" asked Grace.

Wallace opened his backpack. He pulled out a magnifying glass. First, he looked at the acorn. Then he looked at Grace's eye.

Whoa! The magnifying glass made her big owl eye look *enormous.*

"It is!" Wallace pulled out a scavenger hunt list. With a tiny pencil, he crossed out *acorn as big as owl's eye.*

~~Pinecone~~

~~Mushroom with spots~~

~~Acorn as big as owl's eye~~

Red, pointy leaf

Pumpkin seed

Squirmy earthworm

"We found three things," said
Wallace.

"We must find *all* the things,"
said Grace.

The owls in the Great Woods
were having a scavenger hunt. The

first to find everything on the list
would win.

Wallace liked to find things.
Grace liked to win.

They were a good team.

"We need to hurry." Wallace
pointed to the sky. The sun was
starting to rise.

Owls work at night and sleep in
the day.

"Let's go, go, go!" Grace put
the acorn into the backpack. The

pinecone and the mushroom with spots were already inside.

They flew high above the trees. The fall leaves had turned bright yellow, orange, and red.

Whimper, whimper, sniff.

"I hear someone crying," called Wallace. Owls have very good hearing.

"Let's investigate," said Grace. "*Investigate* is a big word for seeing what's wrong."

She liked to use big words.

"I knew *that*." Wallace liked to pretend he knew what her big words meant.

Together, they swooped to the forest floor.

"It's a puppy!" cried Grace. The two owls looked surprised.

The puppy was sad.

The puppy was dirty.

The puppy was smelly. Really, really smelly!

"Why are you crying?" asked Grace.

"I'm lost." The puppy wiped away his tears.

Wallace looked around. No puppies lived in the Great Woods. "Where did you come from?"

"I don't know," said the puppy.

"That's why he's *lost*," Grace explained to Wallace.

"I got that." Wallace turned to the puppy. "What's your name?"

"Jasper. I'm a watchdog."

"Really?" Grace raised her eyebrows. Jasper looked awfully small to be a watchdog. "What do you watch?"

"Apples," said Jasper.

Wallace pulled his notebook out of his backpack. He wrote:

Jasper + apples

A low, grumbling noise burst from Jasper's throat. He leaned toward Wallace.

"Watch out!" Grace stepped back. "The puppy's going to puke!"

"No, I'm not," said Jasper. "I'm *growling*."

"That's your growl?" Grace giggled. "Your growl is not scary for a watchdog."

"I'm not a very good watchdog," admitted Jasper.

"Why did you growl?" asked Wallace.

"I was confused." Jasper pointed to Wallace's pencil. "What are you doing?"

"I'm taking notes. Good detectives take notes," said Wallace.

"You're detectives?" Jasper looked excited.

"We are. We run the Night Owl Detective Agency. We solve mysteries," explained Grace.

"I have a mystery." Jasper panted. "I need you to find my home."

"We need to find a leaf, a seed, and an earthworm," Grace

whispered to Wallace. She had a game to win.

"Let's hear the facts first," said Wallace.

Wallace was all about facts.

"Last night was my first time as watchdog," Jasper told them. "Our family's apples got stolen when my brother and sister were the watchdogs. I wanted to stop the thief."

"Did you?" asked Wallace.

"No." Jasper shook his head.

"The apples were stolen on my watch, too."

"I blame the growl. So not scary," said Grace.

"Who's the apple thief?" Wallace was back to the facts.

"It was dark. I couldn't see them. They put the apples in a sack," said Jasper. "Then they ran away. I chased them, but I didn't catch them. Then I didn't know how to get back home."

"What does your home look like?"
asked Wallace.

"It has a lot of apple trees," said
Jasper.

Wallace tapped his pencil on his
notebook. "More details, please.
Close your eyes. Pretend you are
home. What do you see?"

Jasper closed his eyes. "I see a round face that is always smiling."

"That's nice," said Grace.

"At night, its eyes glow with fire," added Jasper.

"That's scary!" cried Grace. "Where *do* you live?"

"That's what I need to find out. Will you take my case?" begged Jasper.

Grace pulled Wallace to the side. They needed a Partner Talk.

"We can't take his case," said Grace.

"What?" cried Wallace. They had never turned down a mystery before. "Helping a lost puppy is more important than winning." He looked at the sky. "We can wear sunglasses to work in the day."

"It's not that. I want to help, but I can't," said Grace.

Wallace folded his wings. "Why not?"

CHAPTER 2
Begin at the End

"Did you smell that puppy?" Grace covered her beak with her wing. "I refuse to work with him. He needs a bath."

Wallace did not want to miss out on a mystery. "If Jasper cleans up, can we take the case?"

Grace nodded—but kept her wing over her beak.

Wallace led Jasper down a path. Grace flew above them.

"The stink is a clue," Wallace called up to her. "He smells like skunk. That means Jasper met a skunk."

"I fell into a den

of skunks right before I met you," said Jasper. "The skunk babies cried out. Then Mother Skunk gave me a big squirt."

"She wanted to scare you away from her babies," said Grace.

"It worked. I wish I could squirt stink, too," said Jasper.

"You're a dog, not a skunk," Wallace pointed out.

"A *smelly* dog," added Grace.

"We're here." Wallace stopped

next to a swirling river. Two ducks stood by a sign that said: Scrub-a-Duck-Duck. One held a bar of soap. The other held a scrub brush.

"Bath time!" called the ducks.

Jasper groaned. He hated baths. He poked his paw into the water. *Yikes!* It was cold.

"Freeze!" cried Wallace.

"You are wise. It's way too cold for a bath." Jasper quickly pulled out his paw.

"That's not it," said Wallace. "I don't want any clues to wash away. A clue will tell us where you ran last night."

Wallace inspected Jasper with his magnifying glass. He started at the puppy's nose and traveled to his tail.

"*Eeeyoy!*" Wallace pulled a leaf

from Jasper's tail. The leaf was orange with bumpy edges.

"Leaves grow on trees. What was a dog doing up in a tree?" asked Grace.

"The leaves fall down in autumn," Wallace reminded her.

"I ran through a huge pile of leaves, before I met the skunks," said Jasper.

"Was that after the thief took your apples?" asked Grace.

"Yes! I chased the thief into the

woods and then into the leaves. I couldn't find her after that."

Wallace opened his notebook again. "I will write down our clues."

"Let's make a timeline," said Grace. "That will show us the order that things happened last night."

"Great idea." Wallace wrote:

1. Jasper lives by apple trees and glowing face.
2. Jasper chased apple thief into woods.
3. Jasper ran through leaf pile.
4. Jasper was squirted by skunk.
5. Jasper got lost.

"Let's start with clue number one," said Wallace.

"We will look for apple trees," said Grace.

"What about me?" asked Jasper.

"Bath time!" The two ducks gave him a bubble bath.

"Wings in the air! Eyes on the ground," called Wallace. The owls had detective work to do.

"Where do we go?" asked Grace. No apples grew in the Great Woods.

Wallace flew to the right. "There is a swamp this way."

"Apples don't grow in a swamp," said Grace.

Grace flew to the left. "There is a beach this way."

"Apples don't grow on a beach,"
said Wallace.

They flew around and around.

They saw no apples anywhere.

"We need to go backward," said Grace.

Wallace tried to fly backward. His feet flipped over his head. "*Eeeyoy!*" he cried. "This is not a good way to fly."

"I don't want us to fly backward," called Grace. "I want us to solve the mystery by going backward in our timeline."

Now Wallace understood. "We need to retrace Jasper's steps."

They flipped the order of the timeline.

1. Jasper got lost.
2. Jasper was squirted by skunk.
3. Jasper ran through leaf pile.
4. Jasper chased apple thief into woods.
5. Jasper lives by apple trees and glowing face.

"We need to find the skunk," said Wallace. "But how?"

"Follow the stink." Grace
sniffed the ground. She smelled
wet dirt, frog burps, and a bit of
skunk stink—all mixed
together.

"What does your
nose know?" asked
Wallace.

"My nose doesn't
know which way to go." She twirled
around, confused.

"Owls are lousy at smelling."

Wallace pointed to the two tiny nostrils by his beak. "Not much sniffing power."

"I know who has a power sniffer," said Grace.

They hurried back to the river. The ducks dried Jasper with fluffy towels. He smelled like soap.

"We need your super sniffer," said Grace.

Jasper quickly picked up the skunk scent that he had brought through the woods.

He followed it around trees.

He followed it over a log.

He followed it behind a rock—to
the baby skunks.

"Hello again!" Jasper was happy
to see them. He wagged his tail.

Mother Skunk was *not* happy to
see Jasper. She raised her tail.

Jasper growled.

Mother Skunk wasn't scared.

She raised her tail higher.

"Oh no!" cried Grace. They were

all about to be covered in stink.

CHAPTER 3
A Better Idea

Wallace stepped forward. "Please lower your tail. We are here on official business. We are detectives."

"You're Wallace and Grace." Mother Skunk lowered her tail. "Everyone in the Great Woods talks about you."

"They do?" Grace smiled. They were famous!

"We need your help to get this lost puppy back home," said Wallace. "Which way did he come from last night?"

"I'm not sure. It was dark," said Mother Skunk.

"Did you hear a *crunch* or a *squish*?" asked Grace.

Mother Skunk scratched her head. She didn't understand.

"What sound did his paws
make?" Wallace pointed one
way. Acorns covered the ground.
He pointed the other way. Moss
covered the ground.

"Crunch," said Mother Skunk.

They followed the acorns.

Wallace opened his notebook to their backward timeline. "We look for the huge pile of leaves next."

"There are piles under every tree. I'll never get home," moaned Jasper.

"The leaf that was stuck to your tail is our clue. We will match it to the right tree." Grace pulled the leaf from the backpack.

"The leaf is orange," said
Wallace.

"The leaf is bumpy," said Grace.

They flew to the first tree. Grace
picked a leaf. It was orange and
smooth.

"Wrong tree," called Jasper.

They flew to the second tree.
Wallace picked a leaf. It was
bumpy and yellow.

"Wrong tree," called Jasper.

They flew to the third tree.

Grace picked a leaf. It was red and pointy.

"Wrong tree," called Jasper.

"Wait!" cried Grace. "This is the right leaf for the scavenger hunt!" She put the red, pointy leaf in the backpack.

Maybe we can still win, she thought.

They flew to the fourth tree. Wallace picked a leaf. It was orange and bumpy.

"Right tree!" cried Jasper.

They stood by the huge leaf pile under the tree.

"Look! Another clue!" Wallace showed them an apple core. "Someone has been eating apples here."

"Listen up," whispered Grace.

They all heard it: ZZZZZZZZZ.

The leaf pile was making noise!

"You do it," whispered Grace.

"Why me?" whispered Wallace.

"You heard it."

"Do what?" asked Jasper.

"*Shhhh!*" Grace gently lifted a leaf. Then another and another.

A raccoon was fast asleep in the pile! She held an empty sack.

"It's the apple thief," said Jasper.

"That's Sophia," whispered Wallace. They knew her. She

had once stolen berries from the chipmunks.

"Wake her up," said Jasper. "I want my apples back."

Wallace waved the apple core. "Too late for that."

"I have a better idea. Let Sophia sleep." Grace yawned. "We will go to sleep, too."

"Are you serious?" cried Jasper. "What kind of detectives sleep in the middle of a case?"

"Owl detectives," said Grace.
"Sleeping now will help us follow
the trail to get you home."

Wallace thought about what
she'd just said. *Aha!* His partner
had a plan—and Wallace knew
what it was.

He tucked Jasper into a nest on a low branch. The puppy fell asleep right away. He'd been running all night.

Wallace and Grace sat nearby.

"Will your plan work?" asked Wallace.

"I hope so," she said. "We'll know when we wake up."

Then Wallace and Grace both fell asleep.

CHAPTER 4
Tale of the Tail

Rustle, rustle.

Grace opened one eye.

Rustle, rustle.

Grace opened both eyes. The sky glowed orange with the setting sun. Night was on its way.

She listened carefully. Then she

nudged Wallace awake. She put her wing to her beak, so he knew not to speak.

Together, they watched Sophia wake up. She stretched. Then she grabbed her empty sack and left the leaf pile.

Grace shook the puppy. "We need to tail Sophia," she told him.

Jasper grabbed his stubby tail. "No way! I'm not giving her my tail. She has her own."

"*Shhh!*" warned Grace. "*Tail* is a detective word. It means to follow someone without her knowing you are there."

Wallace, Grace, and Jasper tiptoed through the woods. They made sure that Sophia didn't see or hear them.

"Why are we following her?" whispered Jasper.

"She will lead us to your home," said Grace. "I saw her sack was empty. I knew she'd try to steal more apples when it got dark. Sophia is *nocturnal*."

"That's a big word for an animal that sleeps during the day and works at night." Wallace grinned at Grace. He could explain big words, too.

Sophia went around a prickly bush. They went around the prickly bush.

She leaped over a hole. They leaped, too.

Crack! Jasper landed on a twig. He whimpered as it dug into his paw.

Sophia looked behind her.

They hid behind a tree.

She didn't see them. Then Jasper whimpered again.

Wallace
thought quickly.
He gave a loud
hoot to cover
up Jasper's
cries.

Sophia jumped.
She was scared of the
hoot. She hurried on her way.

"That was close," whispered
Grace.

The sky was now dark, but the

moon lit their way. The woods opened into a field. They kept following Sophia.

Suddenly, Grace froze. She pointed ahead. A face glowed in the darkness. Two triangle eyes. A triangle nose. A jagged smile.

Who is that? they wondered.

They watched Sophia wave to the glowing face. Then she ran off.

They moved closer.

"It's a pumpkin," cried Wallace. "Someone carved a face and put a

candle inside. That's the glowing
face."

"Look what I found." Grace held
up a pumpkin seed. "It's on the
scavenger hunt list."

Jasper sniffed the air. "I smell
apples. I smell home!"

Rows of apple

trees stood before them.

"Jasper lives in an apple

orchard," said Wallace.

"We solved the case!" Grace

began to dance. She always danced when they solved a case.

"Oh no! Sophia is stealing more apples." Jasper hurried after her and growled.

Sophia wasn't scared of his growl. She reached for another apple.

"We have to help," said Grace.

Wallace flew across the orchard. In the moonlight, he opened his wings wide. He let out the loudest *hoot.*

Sophia dropped the apple. She shook with fear.

Wallace landed next to her. "Those apples do not belong to you. It is wrong to take them."

"I'm sorry," said Sophia.

"Don't ever come back!" Jasper began to growl, then he looked at Wallace. He had a better idea. He let out a loud *hoot*!

Sophia's eyes went wide. She ran off into the woods, leaving her sack behind.

"You scared her away," Grace told Jasper.

"You're a dog, but you sounded like an owl," said Wallace.

"Now that I can hoot, I will be a great watchdog," said Jasper. "Thank you."

He offered Wallace and Grace big, juicy apples.

Wallace took a bite. An earthworm poked his head out. "Yum!"

"Don't eat him!" Grace rescued the squirmy worm. "You found the last thing on the scavenger hunt list."

Wallace pumped his wing. He liked to find things.

Then he thought about Grace.

"I don't think we won." Wallace frowned. "We took too long to finish."

"That's okay. We solved the case and brought the puppy home." She looked at Jasper with his sisters and brothers. "That's the best kind of winning."

The two detectives flew back to the Great Woods. The apple thief never came back to the orchard again.

She was too scared of the new glowing pumpkin.

READ & BLOOM

PLANT THE LOVE OF READING

Agnes and Clarabelle are the best of friends!

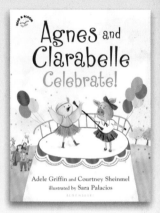

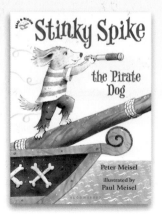

Stinky Spike can sniff his way out of any trouble!

You don't want to miss these great characters!
The Read & Bloom line is perfect for newly
independent readers. These stories are fully
illustrated and bursting with fun!

Caveboy is always ready for an adventure!

Wallace and Grace are owl detectives who solve mysteries!

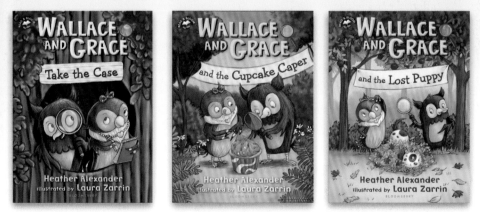

Heather Alexander is the author of many books for young readers, including the Amazing Stardust Friends series. She lives by the woods in New Jersey and often finds deer, fox, turkeys, rabbits, and the occasional owl detective in her yard.

www.heatheralexanderbooks.com

Laura Zarrin is an illustrator by day and a detective by night. She is often called upon to solve mysteries for her family. She's been known to find lost shoes and lost homework and to discover who ate the last chocolate chip cookie. When she's not solving mysteries, she spends her time drawing, reading, drinking really strong iced tea, and eating fig Newtons. She lives in Northern California with her husband, their two sons, and her assistant, Cody the Chihuahua.

www.laurazarrinstudios.com